CITIES
CHICAGO

ABDO
Publishing Company

Nancy Furstinger

visit us at
www.abdopub.com

Published by ABDO Publishing Company, 4940 Viking Drive, Edina, Minnesota 55435.
Copyright © 2005 by Abdo Consulting Group, Inc. International copyrights reserved in all
countries. No part of this book may be reproduced in any form without written permission from
the publisher. The Checkerboard Library™ is a trademark and logo of ABDO Publishing Company.

Printed in the United States.

Cover Photo: Corbis
Interior Photos: Corbis pp. 1, 5, 6-7, 11, 12, 13, 15, 16, 17, 18, 19, 20, 22, 23, 24, 25, 27, 28, 29;
    North Wind pp. 8-9

Series Coordinator: Jennifer R. Krueger
Editors: Stephanie Hedlund, Jennifer R. Krueger
Art Direction & Maps: Neil Klinepier

Library of Congress Cataloging-in-Publication Data

Furstinger, Nancy.
    Chicago / Nancy Furstinger.
        p. cm. -- (Cities)
    Includes bibliographical references and index.
    ISBN 1-59197-857-2
        1. Chicago (Ill.)--Juvenile literature. I. Title.

F548.33.F87 2005
977.3'11--dc22
                                                                2004050949

CONTENTS

CHICAGO

Chicago lies in northeastern Illinois. This is the heart of the Great Lakes region. An ocean of tall prairie grasses once bordered the city. Wind blowing off Lake Michigan rippled across the prairie.

The city stands at the mouth of the Chicago River. The river divides the city into North, West, and South sides. Lake Michigan laps at the shore on Chicago's East Side. This is the largest body of freshwater within the United States. Here, beaches and parks offer outdoor fun.

Chicago has undergone many changes in its long history. Colorful neighborhoods spread out in all directions. Now, a new wave of Chicagoans have moved back to the center of the city. Chicago has grown from a swampy onion patch to a **cultural** center of the Midwest.

Opposite Page: Chicago's Lake Michigan shore provides its citizens with 33 different beaches.

CHICAGO AT A GLANCE

Date of Founding: **1837**

Population: **2,896,016**

Metro Area: **228 square miles (591 sq km)**

Average Temperatures:
- **25° Fahrenheit (-4 °C) in cold season**
- **75° Fahrenheit (24 °C) in warm season**

Annual Rainfall: **33 inches (84 cm)**

Elevation: **579–600 feet (176–183 m)**

Landmarks: **Sears Tower, Lake Michigan**

Money: **U.S. Dollar**

Language: **English**

FUN FACTS

More than 8,000 people visit the Sears Tower every day.

Chicago is home to the DuSable Museum of African American History. It is the first and oldest black heritage museum.

Famous Chicagoans include Maria Shriver, Ernest Hemingway, Walt Disney, former first lady Hillary Rodham Clinton, and Carol Moseley Braun, the first African-American woman elected to the U.S. Senate.

TIMELINE

1673 - Jacques Marquette and Louis Jolliet find a swampy area along what is now Lake Michigan.

1770s - Jean Baptist Point du Sable builds a settlement on the Chicago River.

1803 - The U.S. Army builds Fort Dearborn at the site of Sable's settlement.

1837 - Chicago becomes an official U.S. city.

1848 - The Illinois and Michigan Canal is completed, making Chicago a global port.

1871 - A fire on October 8 destroys much of Chicago.

1886 - The Haymarket Riot kills seven police officers.

1893 - The World's Columbian Exposition is held in Chicago.

1970 - Immigrants arrive from Poland, Germany, and Sweden.

TRADING TOWN

In 1673, French explorers Jacques Marquette and Louis Jolliet found a swampy area along a huge lake. The Native Americans living there called the marsh *Chicagou*, meaning "stinking wild onions."

The Native Americans fished the lake and nearby rivers. In the sea of prairie grasses, they hunted bison and elk. They picked plants for medicine. They also grew corn, squashes, and pumpkins.

Natives swapped their goods with French fur traders. These were the first Europeans to arrive in the area. They hunted for fur and traded with the Native Americans.

Marquette and Jolliet realized a water route connecting the lake with the Mississippi River would control trade.

The first non-native settler was Jean Baptist Point du Sable. He was a fur trapper from the country of Haiti. In the 1770s, he built a cabin at the mouth of the Chicago River.

The U.S. Army felt Sable's settlement was in a key area of the expanding country. So, it sent soldiers there to build Fort Dearborn in 1803. The fort was destroyed at the beginning of the **War of 1812**. Native Americans killed nearly all the soldiers and settlers.

After the war, the fort was rebuilt. The Native Americans were driven west of the Mississippi River. The area around the fort became the village of Chicago in 1833. It continued to grow and became an official city in 1837.

With the increased population, Chicago needed a way to bring supplies to the city. In 1836, workers had started digging a canal. It would be part of a waterway system that would link the Great Lakes with the Mississippi River. The Illinois and Michigan Canal was finished in 1848.

The canal flows about 100 miles (160 km) between the Illinois River and Lake Michigan. It allowed shipments of corn and wheat to enter the city. The canal opened a water route to the center of America. Chicago soon became a global port.

The Illinois and Michigan Canal

Along with its key position on the canal, Chicago was a stop for railroads crisscrossing America in the mid-1800s. Trains brought horses, cattle, and food from the city to the Union army during the **Civil War**. During the war, the demand for pork and beef rose. Chicago's meat plants turned this demand into profit.

Thanks to the river and rail, Chicago underwent a population boom. **Immigrants** from Ireland, Germany, and Scandinavia poured in by boat and train. They worked on the canal, railways, meat plants, and farms.

Chicago also became the world's largest lumber market. Wood processed in Chicago was used to build ready-made houses. The citizens built their houses, shops, docks, sidewalks, and streets with the wood.

FIRE!

On October 8, 1871, a fire started at the O'Leary farm on Chicago's West Side. The city's buildings were all made of

From these ashes, Chicago was rebuilt to become the nation's architectural capital.

wood, and there was a **drought**. So, the fire quickly spread. Three days later, a third of the city had burned. In all, about 18,000 buildings were destroyed and 300 people died.

After the Great Chicago Fire, a new city grew out of the ashes. By 1880, more than 500,000 people called Chicago home. Yet, the newly rebuilt city faced challenges.

One challenge was poor working conditions. In 1886, about 80,000 workers rallied for better treatment. **Scabs** had replaced striking workers at the McCormick Harvester Company. On May 3, workers attacked the scabs. Police attacked the workers, killing one person.

The next night, a rally was held in Haymarket Square. During the rally, a worker threw a bomb. It killed seven police officers. The Haymarket Riot was followed by several attempts to crush the labor movement.

Attention Workingmen!

GREAT

MASS-MEETING

TO-NIGHT, at 7.30 o'clock,

AT THE

HAYMARKET, Randolph St., Bet. Desplaines and Halsted.

Good Speakers will be present to denounce the latest atrocious act of the police, the shooting of our fellow-workmen yesterday afternoon.

Workingmen Arm Yourselves and Appear in Full Force!

THE EXECUTIVE COMMITTEE

Strikers were called to Haymarket Square with this advertisement.

PULLMAN STRIKES

The Haymarket Riot wasn't the only strike in Chicago. In 1894, workers at the Pullman Palace Car Company went on strike. George M. Pullman owned all the buildings his workers lived in. He cut wages at the railroad sleeping car plant. However, rents weren't lowered in the company town. So on May 11, another clash occurred between police and workers. Fortunately, no deaths resulted from the fighting. The strike was then ended, and workers returned to their jobs on August 2.

THE WORLD'S FAIR

Despite its problems, Chicago announced in 1889 that it was the perfect spot to host the World's Columbian Exposition. This fair was to celebrate Christopher Columbus's discovery of the Western **Hemisphere**. New York, St. Louis, and Washington, D.C., also tried to win rights to host the fair.

In 1890, Chicago was chosen as the host city. After three years of preparation, the exposition opened in 1893. It became known as the Chicago World's Fair.

About 27 million people visited the fair. They stepped into a land of fountains, lagoons, canals, and domed buildings. About 65,000 exhibits dotted the grounds from May 1 to October 30.

Fairgoers visited exhibits from around the world. Some featured treasures such as paintings by Pierre-Auguste Renoir, a famous French artist. Others showed off a knight made of prunes, a wax museum, and dwarf elephants!

People spent days exploring the fair. They found fun on the Midway. Here, George Ferris unveiled a wheel that was 250 feet (76 m) high. His Ferris wheel boasted cars that could each hold 60 people. But, the fair's main attraction was Thomas Edison's Tower of Light, which was lit with 18,000 bulbs.

The Ferris wheel at the 1893 World's Columbian Exposition

Chicago's Fair

Chicago hosted a second World's Fair in 1933. This marked the 100th anniversary of the city's founding. The fair's theme was A Century of Progress. Exhibits from the future clashed with the gloom of the Great Depression.

MOVING AHEAD

After the Chicago World's Fair, the city's population continued to increase. City leaders worked to create a transportation system so Chicagoans could get around easily.

Before the fire of 1871, many of Chicago's streets had the same name. This made the search for a home or business

O'Hare International Airport is the busiest airport in the world.

confusing. In 1909, the city adopted a numbering system for the streets. This made it easier for people to locate their destination.

People continued to pour into Chicago. To help them get there, Midway Airport was built in 1923. But, one airport was not enough! In 1942, construction began on O'Hare International Airport. Twenty years later, it became the busiest airport in the world.

Today, Chicagoans enjoy one of the country's best transportation systems. Commuter trains called the Metra bring people into Chicago from the **suburbs**. In the city, people move around on buses. And, they ride the famous elevated train called the L.

The Chicago Transit Authority (CTA) got the name "L" by shortening "elevated." The L runs every 3 to 12 minutes during rush hour. Between the L and buses, the CTA carries more than 1.5 million passengers a day.

MONEY MATTERS

Agriculture has always been an important part of Chicago's **economy**. In 1848, the Illinois and Michigan Canal was used to export corn and wheat. In 1865, the Chicago Union Stock Yards opened. Cattle, hogs, and sheep were shipped here by rail to be butchered.

The Chicago Union Stock Yards polluted the water and air. In 1906, Upton Sinclair was inspired to write **The Jungle.** *It exposed such horrors as sausage made from poisoned rats. The book helped pass a meat inspection law.*

At its prime, Chicago Union Stock Yards processed millions of head of livestock. Armour and Company moved to the stockyards in the 1860s. This pork plant claimed to use every part of the pig but the squeal. Another meat packer, Gustavus Swift, invented a refrigerated railroad car to get his product to market.

The Chicago Board of Trade was founded in 1848. Today, it is part of Chicago's financial district. This district is the second largest in the United States. Only Wall Street is larger.

Today, most of Chicago's citizens work in manufacturing. They make steel, machinery, and leather and agricultural products. Many workers go to jobs in office towers. Company headquarters such as McDonald's, United Airlines, and Sara Lee are located in Chicago.

Tourism is also a large part of the **economy**. Chicago hosts more trade shows, meetings, and **conventions** than any other U.S. city. Tourists also shop along the Magnificent Mile on North Michigan Avenue. This wide street offers popular restaurants, hotels, and fancy shops.

WINDY CITY

Streetcar tracks once looped around downtown. So, citizens began calling that area the Loop. The Loop was home to the first skyscraper in the world. The Chicago skyline rose from the ashes after the fire of 1871. Sandwiched between Lake Michigan and the Chicago River, there was nowhere to build but up.

Today, one of downtown Chicago's most famous sites is the 110-story Sears Tower. It is one of the world's tallest buildings. From its observation deck on the 103rd floor, people can enjoy a view of the third-largest U.S. city.

At 1,454 feet (443 m), the Sears Tower held the title of the world's tallest building from 1974 to 1998.

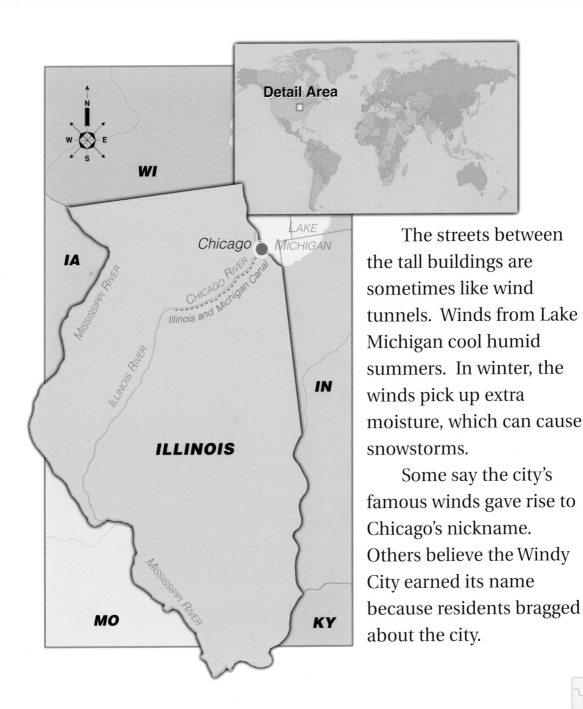

The streets between the tall buildings are sometimes like wind tunnels. Winds from Lake Michigan cool humid summers. In winter, the winds pick up extra moisture, which can cause snowstorms.

Some say the city's famous winds gave rise to Chicago's nickname. Others believe the Windy City earned its name because residents bragged about the city.

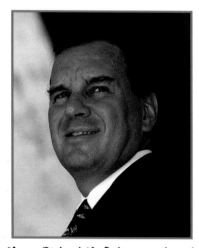

Mayor Richard M. Daley was elected to his fourth term in 1999.

Today's Chicagoans are governed by a mayor along with 50 aldermen. Each alderman represents one of the 50 city wards. The mayor and aldermen are elected every four years.

The elected officials represent a wide range of people. Chicago's population is made of **immigrants**. In 1970, immigrant groups came from countries such as Poland, Germany, and Sweden. Today, the largest **ethnic** group is African American. But, the Hispanic community is growing quickly.

The immigrant groups established communities based on their **culture**. Little Italy, Greek Town, and Chinatown are a few immigrant neighborhoods. Bridgeport and Pilsen are home to Latin Americans. Old Town was settled by Germans, and it is now a well-to-do **suburb**.

These neighborhoods have many types of housing. Some old office buildings and factory lofts are now **condominiums**. People live in city high-rises and single-family houses. Chicagoans also live in bungalows, brick houses, and grand old homes.

Oak Park was once on the edge of a huge prairie. Houses designed by Frank Lloyd Wright grace this area near the Loop.

Chicago's large **immigrant** population means there are many choices of foods. Ribs were brought to Chicago by African Americans. Italians brought pasta, and Greeks serve authentic gyros. Many people also enjoy eating Chicago deep-dish pizza or hot dogs smeared with "the works."

Religion in Chicago is also varied because of the different immigrant groups. Chicago has a large Catholic population. But, there are 119 different religious groups in the city. They include Jewish, Russian Orthodox, and **Islamic** faiths.

It is common to hear several different languages in Chicago. Many immigrants speak in their native languages. However, all business is conducted in English.

English is also the language taught in schools. Children from ages 7 to 16 must attend school. They may attend one of the 550 public schools in Chicago.

Chicago's students study many subjects, including mathematics.

This is the third-largest school system in the United States. Most young students in Chicago go to public elementary and secondary schools. There are also private schools around the city. And, many Roman Catholic schools are available.

Secondary school can include **vocational** and technical high schools. After high school, students can go to one of Chicago's universities. Students enroll at the University of Chicago, Northwestern University, or Loyola University. Several colleges can be found in the **suburbs**, too.

Jane Addams surrounded by children

JANE ADDAMS

Some Chicago neighborhoods in the 1800s revealed a gap between the wealthy and the poor. Rats ran in alleys where children played. One person decided to help the people who lived in these areas.

In 1889, Jane Addams started a settlement house to help the immigrants. That year, she opened Hull House in Chicago's toughest neighborhood. Hull House offered day care, health aid, a variety of classes, and a community kitchen. Addams also brought plays, arts, and concerts to the slums. For her efforts, she received the Nobel Peace Prize in 1931.

DISCOVER CHICAGO

Chicago offers something for everyone. Tourists can explore the city in a range of ways. Trolleys and buses offer tours. Drivers point out landmarks and chat about the city's past.

While the Sears Tower is a must-see, there are many other things to do in Chicago. More than 5,000 years of art can be seen at the world-famous Art Institute of Chicago. And every year, more than 7 million people visit the amusement park at Navy Pier.

At Brookfield Zoo, tourists walk along a squishy swamp filled with native animals such as screech owls. People watch a beehive in action and learn how honey is made at the Chicago Botanic Garden.

Chicago's Museum of Science and Industry is one of the world's most famous museums. There, industry comes alive in the Omnimax theater.

Opposite Page: *The Field Museum of Natural History's anthropology department has more than 600,000 objects! A guide shows students some of the other fossils besides Sue (bottom) at the museum.*

The Field Museum of Natural History displays the skeleton of a Tyrannosaurus rex named Sue. At the push of a button, visitors can hear dinosaurs bellow or smell their breath. At the Chicago Children's Museum, visitors can create airplanes and send them soaring from a 50-foot (15-m) tower.

Wrigley Field's entrance is a Chicago landmark.

Residents and tourists also enjoy sports in Chicago. Two baseball teams call the city home. The Chicago Cubs began in 1876. This team has played at Wrigley Field on the North Side since 1914. On the South Side, the Chicago White Sox play at U.S. Cellular Field. This team was founded in 1900.

Sports fans can catch basketball games at the United Center, where the Chicago Bulls play. This new center also hosts the Chicago Blackhawks ice hockey team.

For football, fans flock to Soldier Field to cheer for the Chicago Bears. This field is also where the Chicago Fire plays major league soccer.

During warm months, boats navigate the Chicago River. Many pass under the Michigan Avenue Bridge, which was the first movable, double-decker bridge ever built.

For those who would rather play than watch sports, Lake Michigan and its parks offer a range of choices. There's fishing, sailing, golfing, running, and biking. Adventure is always blowing through the Windy City.

GLOSSARY

civil war - a war between groups in the same country. The United States of America and the Confederate States of America fought a civil war from 1861 to 1865.

condominium - an apartment that is owned by the tenant and not rented.

convention - a large meeting set up for a special purpose.

culture - the customs, arts, and tools of a nation or people at a certain time.

drought - a long period of dry weather.

economy - the way a nation uses its money, goods, and natural resources.

ethnic - of or having to do with a group of people who have the same race, nationality, or culture.

hemisphere - one half of Earth.

immigrate - to enter another country to live. A person who immigrates is called an immigrant.

Islam - the religion of Muslims. It is based on the teachings of Allah through the prophet Muhammad as they appear in the Koran.

scab - a person hired to replace a striking worker.

suburb - the towns or villages just outside a city.

vocational - relating to training in a skill or trade to be pursued as a career.

War of 1812 - from 1812 to 1814. A war fought between the United States and Great Britain over shipping rights and the capture of U.S. soldiers.

SAYING IT

gyro – YEE-roh
Jacques Marquette – zhahk mawr-keht
Jean Baptist Point du Sable – zhahn BAP-tuhst pwan doo sawbluh
Louis Jolliet – lwee zhawl-yeh
Pierre-Auguste Renoir – pyehr-aw-gyoost ruhn-wawr
Scandinavia - skan-duh-NAY-vee-uh

WEB SITES

To learn more about Chicago, visit ABDO Publishing Company on the World Wide Web at **www.abdopub.com**. Web sites about Chicago are featured on our Book Links page. These links are routinely monitored and updated to provide the most current information available.

INDEX